Howard Weeden

Bandanna Ballads

Howard Weeden

Bandanna Ballads

ISBN/EAN: 9783743306059

Manufactured in Europe, USA, Canada, Australia, Japa

Cover: Foto ©Andreas Hilbeck / pixelio.de

Manufactured and distributed by brebook publishing software
(www.brebook.com)

Howard Weeden

Bandanna Ballads

BANDANNA BALLADS

"AND FANCY HEARS THE ADVENT ROLL
THROUGH THAT OLD NEGRO'S SOUL."

(Page 74.)

Bandanna Ballads

INCLUDING

"Shadows on the Wall"

Verses and Pictures by

Howard Weeden

INTRODUCTION BY JOEL CHANDLER HARRIS

Oh, south winds have long memories.
—EMERSON.

NEW YORK
DOUBLEDAY & McCLURE COMPANY
1899

INTRODUCTION

I AM fortunate indeed in having the opportunity to attach my name, even in a casual way, to the delightful materials out of which this volume is fashioned, for these materials not only possess a vital and an inherent charm of their own, but shed an illumination over all the various efforts, good, bad, and indifferent, that have been made to throw the figures of the old-time plantation negroes on the literary canvas. What has been attempted by many hands wielding the pen is here carried to completion by a woman's hand wielding the brush.

This volume may therefore be said to be the connecting link between the art that is prolix and the art that is precise, between the art that suggests and the art that fulfils. The two arts have met and joined hands

before, but never, so far as I know, under
such satisfactory conditions and with such
complete success; for, as has been intimated,
these memorial portraits illustrate the work
of every conscientious writer who has en-
deavored to depict the character and indi-
viduality of the "quality negroes" familiar
to the Southern plantations before the war—
not only illustrate it, but give it a fresh
claim to consideration.

It is safe to say that never before has an
artist caught with such vital and startling
distinctness, such moving fidelity, the char-
acters which gave to the old plantation, if
not its chiefest charm, at least one of its
most enchanting features. Moreover, these
memorial portraits arrive upon the scene in
the very nick and point of time. A new
generation has arisen, and it has become
incredulous and sceptical in regard to the
traditions and legends of the old plantation
in general, and of the old-time quality negro
in particular. These newcomers find a touch

of romance in the reports that come to them
from their forbears; their curiosity receives
a fillip; they would like to believe in the
substance of what they hear; but they
live in a commercial age, and have a hard
grip on what is practical and concrete.
They look about them for some confirma-
tion of the stories that are told, and they
find not a shred. If there were negroes in
the old days so quaint and gentle, so tender-
hearted and devoted, that novelists and
writers of tales never tire of crowning them
with the halos that are convenient to fiction,
what has become of them? Why have they
disappeared from the face of the earth, leav-
ing no trace behind? Why have they left
no successors? Such is the attitude of an
incredulous generation, engaged in trying to
snatch a few tufts of hair from the seventy-
and-seven thousand prongs of the money-
demon's tail.

Not long ago, a Northern gentleman, who
has been in the South long enough to make

his mark there, wrote to an author of his
acquaintance protesting against the whole-
sale method of making saints of the old-time
negroes. "If you want to display genuine
art," he said, "give it the relish of reality.
Paint the negroes as they now are. When
you do this, I'll take a thousand copies of
your book, and send them broadcast among
my friends in New York and Massachusetts."

Well, the art of Miss Weeden's book is
not only an answer to the sceptical, but is a
welcome and necessary explanation of the
plantation legends that have been preserved.
Whatever the negroes are now, whatever
they may become in the cold-storage conditions of our commercial environment, these
portraits present unimpeachable evidence of
what they were. The art with which the
facts are set forth is so felicitous in its
touch, so faithful and so informing, that it
goes deeper than character and individu-
ality: it revives and resurrects the period;
in some mysterious way it restores the

atmosphere and color of the time. And
each portrait stands out a little masterpiece,
harmonious, powerful, charged with feeling,
and illuminated by the imagination that
makes its creations more real than life itself.
Here are to be found the courtesy, the re-
finement, the dignity, the touch of conde-
scension which the old-time negroes caught
from their masters and mistresses.

Here, too, are portrayed the contradic-
tions that gave relish and zest to the negro
character—independence with loyalty, pride
with gentleness, officiousness with zeal, per-
verseness with graciousness, captiousness
with affection—and the flavor of gentility
which was the result of neither apishness
nor servility. Alas! that the successors and
descendants of these old negroes should
now everywhere answer to the name of
"coons," and that their rich melodies should
be degraded into the vulgar and disgusting
"rag-time" songs!

But, sooner or later, Time will play havoc

with all things over which it claims do-
minion, and in many directions the South
has had a surfeit of such changes as havoc
involves. Therefore I am moved to thank
Heaven for the beautiful genius that has
snatched from the past and preserved the
handful of memories embodied in this book.
For me, and for all who are in love with
simplicity, there is a story behind each pa-
thetic face here pictured, and, indeed, some-
thing of the kind is more than intimated in
the verses that face the portraits—verses that
accompany this symphony of art like a sweet
and softly-played refrain, recurring and filling
up the pauses. In the midst of the furious
striving for effect, characteristic of our brief
day, the simplicity and modesty of these
little poems are very striking. They flutter
across the page as shy and as delicate as the
yellow falling leaves of the mimosa blown
past a dear old lady's window years and
years ago.

JOEL CHANDLER HARRIS.

The Contents

xv

BANDANNA BALLADS

BANDANNA BALLADS

Mammy's Lullaby

"Swing low, sweet Chariot," low enough
   To give some heavenly rest
To dis poor restless little one
   Dat sobs on Mammy's breast.

"Swing low, sweet Chariot," wid your load
   Of angels snowy drest,
And throw a dream out to de chile
   'Most sleep on Mammy's breast.

"Swing low, sweet Chariot," so dat She
   May look into de nest,
An' see how sound her baby sleeps
   At last—on Mammy's breast!

THEOLOGY

Theology

We only had one chile an' hit
We named Theology:
He came on Sunday, so he fit
A Sunday name; besides
De boy was so confusing like
We thought he'd make a preacher,
An' white folks jes' for devilment
Dey called him Little Beecher!

Well, though Theology was smart,
He was dat small an' thin
Dat by an' by he died—an' den
De angels took him in.
Perhaps by time I gits to Heaben
He'll be a growed up preacher
Wid angels givin' him for short
De white folks' name of " Beecher."

OLD TIMES

Old Times

I haven't cooked a 'Possum--Lord!
  For such a long, long time,
It seems to me I've lost somehow
  De very chune an' rhyme.

De times is changed, an' we ain't got
  De consolations which
We're 'bleeged to have if we would cook
  De 'Possum sweet an' rich.

De cabin an' de big fire-place
  Dey neither one is lef'—
With fires so good de 'Possum would
  Almos' jes' cook his se'f.

I ought to think 'bout Canaan, but
  It's Ole Times crowds my mind,
An' maybe when I gits to Heaben
  It's Ole Times dat I'll find!

A CHILD'S EYES

A Child's Eyes

In the dusk of Chloe's rich brown cheek
    The dimples are never at rest,
And bright would the glee of her young face
      be,
    Did not the eyes protest.

Chloe wears her dusky hair
    Twisted, elfin-wise ;
And her face is in bloom with the smiles
    which illume
    All saving her solemn eyes.

And no one knows how the idle face,
    So young and so nearly glad,
Found and hid in its melting eyes
    That Something so deep and sad !

HOMESICK

Homesick

I long to see a cotton field
    Once more before I go,
All hot an' splendid, roll its miles
    Of sunny summer snow !

I long to feel de warm sweet wind
    Blow down de river bank,
Where fields of wavin' sugar cane,
    Are growin' rich an' rank.

I long to see dat Easy World
    Where no one's in a flurry ;
And where, when it comes time to die,
    Dis nigger needn't hurry !

THE INTERPRETER

The Interpreter

The world is a mighty confusin' big place
  For a nigger like me, you know,
An' de only safe thing I have found, has
    been
   To keep a good grip on my hoe !

You can always depend on de fields an' de
    sky
  Whichever way other things go—
An' de res' will get plain in time to de man
  Who keeps a good grip on his hoe !

EVENTIDE

Eventide

A child all wearied with its day
Of laughter, tears, and play,
Is gathered, 'gainst its will, to rest
At eve on Mammy's breast.
She bends above him, dark and calm,
And, tender as a psalm,
She lays a long kiss on his lips,
Till in that soft eclipse
He melts away to sweet release
And sleeps in smiling peace.
Some day I, too, shall go to rest
Upon a kind Dark Breast,
And feel my soul slip through a kiss
As dark and kind—as this!

WHEN MAMMY DIES

When Mammy Dies

We're always young till mammy dies ;
But when her hand no longer lies
As once it did upon our head
We feel that youth with her has fled.

We watch her wing her way to Rest,
And see ourselves upon her breast,
Our young selves—cradled as of yore—
Now borne from us forevermore.

We hear their last faint lullaby
Blown softly backward from the sky,
And as they soar beyond our reach
We wave farewell to each, to each !

MOTHER AND MAMMY

Mother and Mammy

Among the ranks of shining saints
  Disguised in heavenly splendor,
Two Mother-faces wait for me,
  Familiar still, and tender.

One face shines whiter than the dawn,
  And steadfast as a star;
None but my Mother's face could shine
  So bright—and be so far!

The other dark one leans from Heaven,
  Brooding still to calm me;
Black as if ebon Rest had found
  Its image in my Mammy!

THE OLD BOATMAN

The Old Boatman

I changed my name, when I got free,
    To "Mister" like the res',
But now dat I am going Home,
    I likes de ol' name bes'.

Sweet voices callin' "Uncle Rome,"
    Seem ringin' in my ears;
An' swearin' sort o' sociable,
    Ol' Master's voice I hears.

De way he used to call his boat,
    Across de river: "Rome!
You damn ol' nigger, come an' bring
    Dat boat, an' row me home!"

He's passed Heaven's River now, an' soon
    He'll call across its foam:
"You, Rome, you damn ol' nigger, loose
    Your boat, an' come on Home!"

AUNT JUDY AND THE PAINTER

Aunt Judy and the Painter

I can't allow my picture took
  De way you wants to draw—
A-leavin' off my Freedom-look
  For fashions 'fore de war.

You'd have my dress, you say, "be plain,
  Of dat dull quiet blue,
Dat caught from years of sun and rain,
  Its tender faded hue."

An' on my "head a turban red
  Worn wid a stately grace—"
"To harmonize—" I think you said,
  "Wid my rich, dark brown face."

No, Lord! my picture can't be caught
  By man wid no sich manners;
Dat's 'zactly why de war was fought—
  To end dem same bandannas!

TWO LOVERS AND LIZETTE

Two Lovers and Lizette

Who, me? in love, an' wid Lizette?
 You better b'lieve I ain't ;
No sassy gal like dat could give
 Dis nigger heart-complaint.

If Gord don't love her more den I,
 Den all I got to say
Is, dat her soul's in danger sho',
 An' she had better pray !

It's her, dat is in love wid me ;
 An' I jes laughs an' tell her,
"De fruit dat draps d'out bein' shook
 Is sho' to be too meller !"

But all de same, you talks too much
 To suit me, 'bout Lizette :
Some gent'man's nigger gwine get hurt
 About dat same gal yet !

THE BANJO OF THE PAST

The Banjo of the Past

You ax about dat music made
   On banjos long ago,
An' wants to know why it ain't played
   By niggers any mo'.

Dem banjos b'longed to by-gone days
   When times an' chunes was rare,
When we was gay as children—'case,
   We didn't have a care.

But when we got our freedom, we
   Found projeckin' was done ;
Our livin' was to make—you see,
   An' dat lef' out de fun.

We learned to vote an' read an' spell,
   We learned de taste ob tears—
An' when you gets dat 'sponsible,
   De banjo disappears !

POSSUM TIME

'Possum Time

When autumn skies are deeper blue
Than any skies June ever knew;
When frost has touched the mellow air
Till yellow leaves fall everywhere;
When wild grapes scent the wind with wine,
And ripe persimmons give the sign,
Then Life seems happy as a rhyme
Because—it's nearly 'Possum time!

When fires roar on the cabin-hearth,
And ovens bubble low in mirth;
When sweet potatoes slowly bake,
And Mammy makes her best ash-cake;
When Daddy climbs the "jice" and throws
A string of peppers down, it shows,
That Life is happier than a rhyme,
Because at last—it's 'Possum time!

TOO LATE

Too Late

Yes, Master, dat's jes' what I think :
   Dat Freedom is first rate.
I only means to say it came
   For some of us, too late !

De days dat you call "slavery days"
   Seemed happy ones, you see,
Becase I was so young an' gay
   An' Dinah was wid me.

But jes' as Freedom come along
   My Dinah up an' died ;
An' I got ol' an' couldn't learn
   De new ways, dough I tried.

So when dey talks 'bout being free,
   An' I don't seem to heed 'em,
You may jes' know my heart's brimful,
   An' tears has drownded Freedom !

A STUDIO DISPUTE

A Studio Dispute

In vain my palette bears a score
  Of browns, and yellows, too ;
In vain I ask of other eyes
  What is my model's hue ?

" A glow from Afric suns," I cry,
  " Still lingers in her face,
And keeps a light there, as if flame
  Shone through an amber vase ! "

A Poet near my easel thinks
  Her color-scheme was laid
By that old Singer who once called
  A girl " The Nut-Browne Mayde."

Old Remus looks to where she sits,
  Posing with half-turned head,
And says : " You gent'men bof is wrong,
  Dat gal is ginger-bread ! "

A REGRET

A Regret

Dar's always somethin' wantin'
  In my joy at bein' free,
When I think ol' Master didn't
  Live to share dat joy with me.

Dem was mighty big plantations
  Dat he owned before de war
An' he, de kindes' master
  Dat darkies ever saw.

But de care of dem was heavy,
  Makin' him de slave, not we—
An' often I have heard him say
  He wished dat he was me!

An' if he jes' was livin',
  He would have his wish, you see—
Dem niggers couldn't own him now,
  An' Master would be free.

BEATEN BISCUIT

Beaten Biscuit

Of course I'll gladly give de rule
    I meks beat biscuit by,
Dough I ain't sure dat you will mek
    Dat bread de same as I.

'Case cookin's like religion is—
    Some's 'lected, an' some ain't,
An' rules don't no more mek a cook
    Den sermons mek a Saint.

Well, 'bout de 'grediances required
    I needn't mention dem,
Of course you knows of flour and things,
    How much to put, an' when ;

But soon as you is got dat dough
    Mixed up all smoove an' neat,
Den's when your genius gwine to show,
    To get dem biscuit beat !

Two hundred licks is what I gives
    For home-folks, never fewer,
An' if I'm 'spectin' company in,
    I gives five hundred sure !

A PLANTATION HYMN

A Plantation Hymn

Far down the west still glows the light,
Though elsewhere it is night.
The fields are quiet as the stars,
Save some one at the bars
Whose full heart, quivering to the brim.
Flows over in a hymn.
It sends its strangely solemn tide
Of Hallelujahs, wide—
Across the fields, and up as far
As to the fartherest star,
Till all the Southern night's in bloom
With Song and Star-sown gloom--
And Fancy hears the Advent roll
Through that old negro's soul !

A Banjo Song

I plays de banjo better now
   Dan him dat taught me do,
Becase he plays for all de worl'
   An' I jes' plays—for You.

He learns his chunes—I jes' lets down
   A banjo string or two
Into de deepest of my heart,
   An' draws up chunes for You.

Slowly dey comes swingin' up
   A-quiverin' through and through,
Till wid a rush of tinglin' notes
   Dey reaches light—an' You.

I never knows if dey will shine
   Wet wid tears or dew;
I only knows dat, dew or tears,
   Dey shine becase of You.

THE BORROWED CHILD

The Borrowed Child

My chile ?   Lord no, she's none o' mine,
    She's des one I have tried
To put in place of Anna Jane—
    My little one what died.

Dat's long ago ; no one but me
    Knows even where she lies :
But in her place I've always kept
    A borrowed chile, her size.

As soon as it outgrows my chile,
    I lets it go, right straight—
An' takes another in its place
    To match dat Heabenly mate.

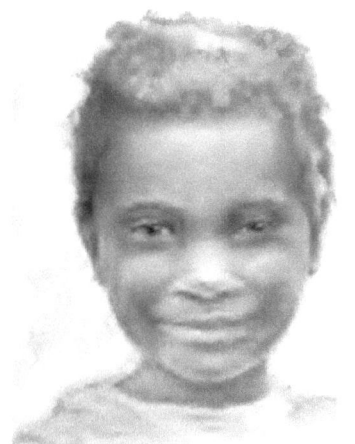

The Borrowed Child

It's took a sight o' chillun, sho',
  To ease dat dull ol' pain,
An' keep de pretty likeness fresh
  Of my dead Anna Jane.

Der's more den forty years, you see,
  Since she has been in Heaben,
But wid de angels years don't count—
  So she's still only seben.

Time treats us all up dere, des lak
  It do white ladies here—
It teches 'em so light—one's still
  A gal at forty year!

THE DEVIL'S GARDEN

The Devil's Garden

On Master's ol' plantation, where
    I lived before de war,
A field called " Devil's Garden " was
    De worst you ever saw.

De work right dere it was so hard
    We knew de Devil made it ;
And often found a hoof-track dere
    Where he had been an' laid it.

When Freedom came I wanted ease ;—
    So off from dere I put ;
But somehow every job I've tried
    Has showed de cloven-foot !

EASY LIVING

Easy Living

Dar's two times in de year dat Gord
   Made for de nigger sho',
Two times when he's so rich he don't
   Ask Gord for nothin' mo':

Blackberry time is one; for den
   He neither hoes nor sows;
De nigger knows his daily bread
   Right on de bushes grows.

De other's Watermilion time;
   An' den—Lord bless your soul!
Bof bread an' water grows for him,
   In one big cool green bowl!